Another Little How to Book
How to stay married to your man

By:
Sherri Hill

Trafford PUBLISHING® www.trafford.com
North America & international
toll-free: 1 888 232 4444 (USA & Canada)
fax: 812 355 4082

This book is dedicated to my
"Girls"

Another Little How to Book

How to stay Married to Your Man

Contents

Prologue

Okay ladies here is another how to book. This book is for the married female, or the female that has decided to live with her mate. Some things you may agree with others you may not, but remember this book is solely based on my opinion, experiences, and conversations that I have had with others; that are married to, or living with that significant other, none of it is law. I have given this much thought and have decided that maybe I have the insight to make this thing work not only for myself but for others.

Give It Some Thought

Chapter 1

Give It Some Thought

It takes time to get to know a person, to find out whether or not you have things in common and longer to accomplish the same goals. Keep in mind that you do not choose a mate with the intent of changing him as a person, but with the intent to combine your two personalities to make a whole.

You need to remember what attracted you to that person. Was it their physical strength, spiritual or character strength? Was it the way he made love? Was it his ability to be straightforward? Was it his drive when it came to making money? You should remember what it was about this person that attracted you to him in the beginning. You must also have a clear understanding of why you are getting married, or moving in with this person. Is it just the sex? Is it just the money? If you are marrying for superficial reasons then regardless of what you try; it is destined to fail.

Compromise

Chapter 2

Compromise

We must remember that there are no perfect people out there. This is not to say that you should settle for anything; remember, you are not perfect and someone has to put up with your little idiosyncrasies *(habits, faults, and your shit)*.

Often times, we try to force our opinions, life style, if you will where they cannot be forced. When you marry or move in with a mate remember all bets are off. We are individuals with very different personalities.

Consider that the vast majority of the male population is raised by a single female and is taught very early that he should be the bread winner, head of the household, protector. Although, you may call this man baby he is by no means a baby. Men are supposed to be a forceful presence, and depending upon what position he holds in his line of siblings, he may have been brought up to have a presence very much like that of his father *(very dominant.* They are also taught to be hard not to display too much emotion in front of a woman, or he will appear soft. We all know that men have trouble with public displays of affection. Society places a heavy burden upon men. They are taught from the time they are very young that women are women and men are men, the protector, provider, and the bread winner. (I *cannot stress this enough*)

Never look for this man to say that he is sorry, because he will not. He will though, cook your favorite food, take you out to dinner at your favorite restaurant, or keep the kids so that you can have the day off. Allow this man to apologize in his own way. All of these things are apologies. Accept them, if you love and care about this man then move on, because this life is to short for the *madness.*

Never think that you will win an argument striking head on. The best way to deal with an argument is to not let it happen. Yes, you have an opinion but it is best presented softly when you are lying in bed or curled up talking. He will not hear you if you are shouting, cursing, and forcing your opinion down his throat.

The next time you have an argument present it softly, if he says the he is through with the argument, present it later in a different way. There is always a way to get your point across. Try presenting it while taking a bath together. You have a lot of options open to you, use them. You are female use it. (*Hello*)

Never look for this man to be overly affectionate in public. He will not. It is not in his personality; but at home cuddle if you want, sit in his lap, lie on his shoulder, kiss him if thats what you want to do. Run a bath for the two of you, join him in the shower. He won't say no; you are his wife, mate or significant other. If he won't kiss you, kiss him. Understand that this man shows you how much he loves you every time he makes love to you. Notice that while he may be a quiet lover; he is intense and passionate making sure all of your needs are met. Again remember this life is too short for the *madness.*

I do not think that as women we understand how much power we actually have. The power in being female is awesome. We cannot handle our lives at home as we do our lives at work. Yes, you are a big time corporate lawyer, a doctor, a director, supervisor, general in the army, but at home you are a wife and a mother. The nurturing has to come from you. Give in to your feminine side love your mate and your children, with all the passion you are capable of.

Keep in mind this is the man you vowed to love, cherish and respect until death do you part. So do not be so quick to throw in the towel at the start of trouble.

Alright ladies all marriages have problems, money bad habits, (*Shit happens*), but does this mean that you throw in the towel. What if it were you? Should you be forgiven for your bad habits? You can't throw in the towel at the first sign of trouble you have to have the strength to work though it. Marriages are supposed to have strength. Marriages are supposed to be able to withstand some (*Shit*) being thrown at them. Talk it out but do not nag.

Please do not take advice from your friends about your marriage. Do not listen to your *man less friends*, because what are they using for a reference point. They do not have a man. Why do you think that they are single? Forgive me, if your friend tells you she can have a man whenever she wants, please ignore this comment, because if she could she would have one. She would not need to feed off of the things that go on in your life. Do not listen to your *unhappily* married friend; remember *misery loves company.*

Cooking and Getting Along

Chapter 3

Cooking and Getting Along

Cooking; why not learn to cook? For no other reason than to feed you, fast food is not a dietary supplement. Cooking can bring couples together. Let us imagine for a minute that your only perfect dish is salad, well if he cooks dinner then you make your perfect salad. Find out what his favorite foods are and how to prepare them, even if you totally mess them up he will be more than pleased with your efforts.

Ask his mother or sisters what his favorite foods are and how to prepare them. Get to know them you will find that they love you as much as he does. They are the perfect *allies* when trouble rears its ugly head. They will always be on your side to help you through any major mess.

Children

Chapter 4

Children

Children, if this man has children accept them; because you would want him to accept yours. Children are our most precious commodity, and he loves them more than he loves himself. So do not be so selfish that you cannot love a child. No, it is not easy but it can be done.

Ladies stop to consider that you may have children. How many times have you said that a man has to accept you and your children? How many times have you told a girlfriend that you would not be bothered with a man with children, but then you have them? I cannot have a man taking away money from my children, but isn't that, the responsibility of their biological father and you. Then my question to you is again why does he have to accept your children but you do not have to accept his? How selfish is this?

Friends

Chapter 5

Friends

Friends, okay ladies you cannot pick his friends. It simply does not work. It doesn't matter how immature, corrupt, idiotic, or morally bankrupt you think they are. He has to come to realize that they are not good for him in his own time. If you persist in telling him whom he can and cannot associate with, you will make the situation worse. He will be determined to keep them as friends.

You may have friends that he does not like, but you would not allow him to tell you that you could not hang with your girls. How dare he tell you who you can and cannot have as friends? Okay ladies, how many of your girls try to tell you not to go home to your man. Remember these so called friends may have their *eye on your man*, or *no man at all*, or a *relationship that is crap*. Girl you do not hang with us like you use to *(how many times have you heard this?)* I will not have a man define who I am. How many times have you heard this? Let us stop and think for a minute. How many relationships has that particular friend had fail? How many men does she hang with? Does she have any one stable in her life; not a *Booty call*, but someone that loves and cares about her? Think about it.

Family

Chapter 6

Family

Family, trust that this man loves his family more than anything in the world; his wife and children, but also remember that he loves his mother, sisters, and brothers. *Mother-in laws and sisters;* you should try and get along with the women in his family. He loves these women and would do anything for them.   Do not think that he is ignoring you. Do not make him choose between his love for you and the love he has for his family. If you have married the eldest male of a family he is everyones favorite and everyone looks up to him, and he has a certain obligation to his family.

Oh yes, just stop and think for a minute, would you allow anyone to tell you that you could not spend time with your mother, hang with your sister or help your baby brother if he had a few problems? You love your family. Let us try and be understanding *Hmmmmmmmm.* It is completely okay for you to need family that you love and care about; but not him. How many times have you told your girls; I wish he would try and stop me from seeing my mother or taking care of my father, or my family? How many times have you argued with this man, when your family needed something, and you were going to give it to them regardless of how he felt? Now consider when he wants to help his family how much drama do you give him?

You love your mother, sisters, and brothers. Never try to tell him that he cannot spend time with his mother, sisters, or brothers. Ladies, and if he has other children please try not to give him drama. He has enough *baby mama drama*, he does not need it from you too, remember he married you. He lives with you.

Cheating

Chapter 7

Cheating

Cheating, let us talk about cheating for a minute. It is one of the major causes of divorce in America. It has happened to men in the public eye, as well as men not so in the public eye. I am going to say "Shit happens". I am not saying condone it; give the brother a break or at least the benefit of the doubt. You make sure he knows how this will not be tolerated, and how much he has damaged the trust that you had in him. If you forgive him for his bad habit, let it go do not bring it up again because it is in the past; and for goodness sake stop nagging. The best way for people to see themselves is to say nothing at all. He can't see himself if you won't shut up.

Definitely two wrongs do not make a right, so before you retaliate and try to inflict as much hurt as you are feeling stop and think. Is it worth it? What will it cost you? What will you lose? You are female; do not hang yourself out there like that remain a lady. Do you really want to give your man to some other woman that might have been just a fling? There are always options; counseling, your pastor, your mother, and a good friend with a strong spiritual and emotional foundation. If it were you would you want him to leave you or forgive you? I would think that you would want forgiveness. After you forgive this man forgive yourself, it is not your fault and it is in the past and do not bring it up again. Seek out counseling.

Married Men

Chapter 8

Married Men

*L*et us talk about married men for a minute. Okay this is a problem for most women. Lets try and pay attention. If you can only call him on his cell phone, guess what he is not busy he belongs to *someone else* or is *Married*. If you can never attend any of his family functions but he always comes to yours, guess what he is *MARRIED or living with someone*. If you can only meet a few of his friends and he never takes you out in public, guess what he is *MARRIED or living with someone.* If you can never spend the night and wake up in his bed guess what he is not your *MAN. He is married or living with someone.*

When the holidays roll around if he can only drop by for a few minutes and has to hurry away, or comes by the next day claiming something came up; do I have to say it? *HE IS MARRIED or living with someone.* If you give him a ride home and must drop him a block from his home, the neighborhood is not dangerous he does not want his wife or live in mate to see you. If he is always unavailable for important dates, you never go on trips together, you can only call him at work, or on the cell phone, and you can only text him and wait for a call back; guess what *MARRIED or living with someone.*

Now let me clear up a few things that you might have misunderstood. The things that you are told about his miserable home life, do not believe them; a man with all of this misery would be single.

Please ignore all of the horrible things that he says he has to put up with, and that he is only staying in the relationship for the children. He is there because that is where he wants to be. He is not going to jeopardize his life with his wife and children for you. When he tells you oh baby I am planning to divorce her, please do not believe this. This man is not only greedy but selfish and a liar. He wants his life with his family and his life with you. I hope that this has cleared up a few things. Ladies lets stop the *DENIAL,* and *ADMIT THE OBVIOUS.* Let us please pay attention to the facts.

Ladies if you are married to one of these men that are greedy and selfish, and cannot correct his behavior and become a family man through counseling and spiritual advising then you know what to do.

Lying

Chapter 9

Lying

Lying is another problem not tolerated in a relationship remember brothers trust is a hard thing to come by and once it is lost it is hard to regain. Sisters understand that if you back some one in a corner that person may lie. How many times have we as women told a little lie to get something that we really wanted? Think about it, it is all lying. I am not saying accept it; find out why the truth is a problem for this man. Help him work through his problem of not being able to tell the truth. Explain to him how lying destroys the foundation of a good marriage or relationship. It really destroys the foundation of one that has had to withstand a lot of drama.

Not Your Maid

Chapter 10

Not Your Maid

This man is not a maid. A lot of women marry because they think that a man will do whatever is asked, if he wants to keep her. Not true, people in general when they care about another person are more than willing to meet all of that persons needs. Do not think for a moment that this man is weak because when pushed he will leave. He will find another mate that is as giving as he is. Please do not think for a minute that it is acceptable to take advantage of anyone. Would you want someone to take advantage of you? This man is not your maid. The sex is great not because of size or talent, where these things may be important, most men are very passionate about the women that they love.

Do not think for one minute that as a man, this man will work two jobs, give you his money, take care of the house, your kids, make love to you and kiss your ass too. In a relationship there has to be some give and take from both sides.

Domestic Violence vs. An Argument

Chapter 11

Domestic Violence vs. an Argument

Domestic violence vs. an argument, all right here is where it becomes intense. An argument is the one thing that is easily worked out; time apart from each other can cure this ill; a walk to sort things out, a movie, to relax and think some soft music, so everyone can calm down or maybe a quiet dinner. *"This one was easy".*

This topic is tougher; I do not believe anyone should be verbally or physically abused. We have to draw the line somewhere. Women; we have to learn that when an argument gets really heated to back down, regroup and try another tactic. Men; you have to learn to check your temper. Walk it off if you have to, go for a ride, talk to a friend, or go in another room. Ladies do not follow someone around who is trying to manage his anger.

Couples must learn to manage their anger. If none of this works, and an argument results in a fist fight, with you being at the opposite end of the fist, *then yes it is time to leave.* Sometimes you must walk away to protect you, and your children. Seek counseling so that you understand it is not your fault he is abusive. The same applies for verbal abuse. It is time to leave before it becomes unbearable. These things have to be worked out through counseling and anger management.

Cell Phones

Chapter 12

Cell Phone

Cell phones, okay these are Lojacks in disguise you know a locator, a means to keep track. Let the man call you. He is not being jealous but protective. Remember this is one of the qualities that attracted you to this man in the first place. He is strong, a good provider, a passionate lover, and yes your protector. So allow him the luxury of calling you. You are not offended when you speak to the same girlfriend ten times a day. You know the one. The one that has no life and is always in your business; telling you what she would not take off of a man, but has no man, you know her.

General Crabbiness

Chapter 12 1/2

General Crabbiness

General crabbiness, when you notice that either you are crabby or your man is crabby, the best way to fix this is a little space. Sometimes he has had a bad day, or not enough sleep. He is hungry, or the major cause of crabbiness he just might be horny, *and you know how to handle this one"*. Sometimes he has something on his mind. It is amazing what a nap can still cure, or just some time spent apart. A few hours is not a lot of time, and is time well spent apart if it avoids an argument. Ladies we all know that when *PMS* hits which generally makes us crabby; we tend to become confrontational. Give the man his space.

Laziness

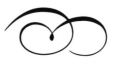

Chapter 12 3/4

Laziness

Let us discuss this for a minute. I am not talking about folding clothes, or putting them in the laundry basket. This has nothing to do with him taking the garbage out right when you suggest it, or mowing the lawn. He will do these things with out you telling him.

I am talking about an unemployed man, a man that is unemployed by choice; not one who became unemployed through a layoff, or downsizing. I am not, speaking of the man that has lost his job because the company went out of business. I am though, speaking of the man whom as a young man had no goals, aspirations, or ambitions. The one who blamed his inability to excel on everyone but himself, you know the one.

When you met him he had a car, (*not his own but his moms*) and lived with his mom but no job to speak of. His mom kept the car full of gas. He was not in school, unemployed and not trying to find a job or get in school. He is the one that has an excuse for everything, why he can't find a job, why he can't help his mom, and why he is not in school. Leave this *zero* at home with his mom he is never going to change. His mom has had a hand in enabling this behavior. Ladies do not confuse sex with love. They are not the same (*Do not further enable this man*).

Please think all males function the same; what one will not do another one will. If you see that this man is not productive and not trying to be, do not think that if you marry him he will change. He will not change. You will end up with a *zero* for a husband. One that expects you to work while he tells you why he cannot, a man who has replaced his moms car with yours, remember *any man can give you a wet ass.* You will in the end be responsible for supporting this man. You need a man with some bite, a man that can be there when you fall. A man with some grit, understand it does not matter how many times this man has fallen, what matters is how he gets up after he has fallen.

Selfishness

Chapter 12 7/8

Selfishness

*L*adies lets not just be reasonable but understanding as well. If you have a mate that has taken care of your every need, and all of a sudden falls on hard times ladies, ladies, ladies, let us stop and think. Do not abandon this man when he needs you the most. It is your turn to pick up the slack (*help a brother out*). We all know you are the last person he wants to ask for help. A man feels soft if he has to ask his woman for help. Ladies because if this does not seem like the reasonable compassionate answer for the man that you profess to be in love with; then I have just one thing to say *SELFISH;* let us not be selfish.

Epilogue

Remember ladies you are the backbone of the family for without you the family would fall apart. You are the disciplinarians, cooks, cleaning ladies, doctor, night nurse, nurturer, referee, director, business partner, lover, friend, companion, mother and yes wife and mate. You manage bills with the skill of an accountant. You tackle problems with the analytical skill of a strategist.

Yet somewhere along the way we have learned to be critical, unforgiving and hard. We are compassionate, loving individuals and should never forget it. Take the time to appreciate each other for this life is shorter than either you or I think. Life is too short for the *madness*.

On a personal note in case none of this works, and PMS is totally in control put this book in a safe place; do not use it as a weapon and handle your business.

Acknowledgments

This book would have not been possible without the extraordinary support of a number of people. I have to begin with my husband Hector and son Garth; living with an author is bad enough, being married to an author that Substitute teaches while writing a book requires the patience of Job. I understand more fully just how lucky I am to have my husband and son in my life.

I want to express as well my gratitude to my friends; Joy, Doris and Jackie. I would also like to thank my cousins Miss J. and Judy for going beyond the call; it's made a world of difference.

Printed in the United States
By Bookmasters